chat

book one

nan mccarthy

RAINWATER PRESS

for pat

When I wrote *Chat* in 1995 (and *Connect* & *Crash* in '96 & '97), online communication was still unfamiliar to a lot of people—which is why *Chat, Connect, & Crash* featured a glossary to explain all the "new" acronyms and emoticons like LOL and ;-). Although such terms and symbols are now ubiquitous, I decided to keep the glossary in the new edition (which you can find at the back of the book) to retain the flavor of the original books.

I self-published a print edition of *Chat* in 1995, following up with printed copies of *Connect* in 1996. *Chat* was the first full-length email epistolary novel ever written, and among the earliest novels sold online directly to readers. (For a more detailed publishing timeline of the trilogy, visit www.nan-mccarthy.com.) By the time I wrote the third book in the series—*Crash*—in 1997, the books were getting notice in *The New York Times*, *The Wall Street Journal*, *Glamour*, and *People*.

When Simon & Schuster bought the rights to the trilogy— publishing *Chat, Connect, & Crash* in trade paperback in 1998—they requested a different ending to *Crash* than the one that appeared in the original manuscript. In 2012 I acquired the rights to the trilogy back from S&S and now, in 2014, the trilogy is once again self-published and features the original ending to *Crash* as it was first written.

Aside from the restoration of the ending, most of the original text has been left intact. I've done some editing for a smoother and better reading experience (such as shortening the email headers), and I added more detail in some key scenes. *Chat, Connect, & Crash* are a snapshot of the emerging online culture of the 1990s, but the story of Bev and Max and their relationship is, I hope, timeless.

Nan McCarthy
2014

Name: Beverly J.
ID: BevJ@frederic_gerard.com
Location: Midwest
Birthday: October 11
Sex: Female
Marital Status: Married
Computer(s): Mac Quadra 650 and PowerBook 150
Interests: Reading, playing the piano, typography
Occupation: Editor
Favorite Quote: "Great works are performed not by
    strength but by perseverance." — *Samuel Johnson*

Name: Maximilian M.
ID: Maximilian@miller&morris.com
Location: Planet Earth
Birthday: Taurus
Sex: Male
Marital Status: single
Computer(s): who cares
Interests: bonsai gardening, writing poetry, mixing the
    perfect martini
Occupation: copywriter
Favorite Quote: "For myself I live, live intensely and am
    fed by life, and my value, whatever it be, is in my own
    kind of expression of that." — *Henry James*

Friday, July 14, 1995 1:48 a.m.
From: Maximilian@miller&morris.com
To: BevJ@frederic_gerard.com
Subj: Hello

Beverly, (is that your real name?)

I've seen your messages in the Writers' Forum and you seem to know a lot about computers. I'm thinking of upgrading my old '386 PC and I'm wondering if you can give me any advice on whether I should buy a PC or a Mac.

Also, I noticed in your member profile you're an editor.

Where do you work? I'm a copywriter . . . maybe we could get together sometime.

Maximilian (that's my real name)

Monday, July 17, 1995 7:32 a.m.
From: BevJ@frederic_gerard.com
To: Maximilian@miller&morris.com
Subj: Thanks, but No Thanks

Maximilian:

I really don't like to give advice on whether a person should buy a Mac or a PC, especially because I know nothing about the way you work and what you want to accomplish with your computer. If you're just going to be doing word processing, it probably doesn't matter which computer you use.

I'm sorry I don't have time to chat but I'm under a deadline at the moment.

p.s. In case you didn't notice, my member profile says I'm married.

Monday, July 17, 1995 11:08 a.m.
From: Maximilian@miller&morris.com
To: BevJ@frederic_gerard.com
Subj: Ouch!

Sheesh! You didn't seem so uptight in your messages on
the Writers' Forum. Besides, I wasn't trying to pick you
up—I don't do cybersex, and you could be a real toad for
all I know.

I promise to quit bugging you if you'll just tell me if
Beverly is your real name.

Maximilian

Tuesday, July 18, 1995 6:50 a.m.
From: BevJ@frederic_gerard.com
To: Maximilian@miller&morris.com
Subj: Re: Ouch!

Maximilian:

Excuse me? I am not a toad, for your information. You, on
the other hand, are probably wearing a smelly jogging suit
with your butt hanging out the back and Cheetos crumbs
stuck to your beard.

But since you've promised to stop bothering me, I will tell
you that Beverly is my real name. And I am *not* uptight,
BTW.

Beverly

Beverly,

Look, I'm really sorry. I had a hangover when I wrote that
message at work yesterday morning. Can we start over?
I swear I wasn't trying to pick you up . . . I've just been a
copywriter for so long I was curious how you got to be an
editor.

Maximilian

p.s. I don't wear jogging suits, I don't have a beard, and I
don't even like Cheetos. What does BTW mean? And why
did you put asterisks around one of your words?

Wednesday, July 19, 1995 7:23 a.m.
From: BevJ@frederic_gerard.com
To: Maximilian@miller&morris.com
Subj: Re: Sorry

Maximilian:

I thought you said you wanted computer advice, not career
advice? And who's your boss anyway? From the time on
your messages, it looks as if you're strolling into work just

in time to take your lunch break. If you worked for me, I'd
fire your ass in a heartbeat.

Beverly

p.s. You must be new online—BTW stands for "by the
way." People use all sorts of acronyms like that to make
typing online faster and easier. The asterisks are used for
emphasis, since you can't type in italics in email. Some
people use underscores (_like this_) to mean the same
thing.

Thursday, July 20, 1995 11:41 a.m.
From: Maximilian@miller&morris.com
To: BevJ@frederic_gerard.com
Subj: Re: Sorry

OK, so now that we've established we could never work
together I guess there's not much else to talk about, since
you seem fairly incapable of having any kind of conversa-
tion that's even remotely personal.

(And yes, I'm new to this whole online thing.)

Maximilian

Friday, July 21, 1995 8:02 a.m.
From: BevJ@frederic_gerard.com
To: Maximilian@miller&morris.com
Subj: Truce?

Maximilian,

I am not incapable of participating in friendly discussion.
It's just that I get a lot of weird emails from people I don't
even know. Usually people want something from me,
like they want me to read their nephew's first novel and
help him get it published, or they want computer advice
(ahem), or sometimes people are just plain lunatics and I
have to change my email address in order to get away from
them. One woman found out where I live and started calling me at all hours of the night, wanting to talk about her
novel-in-progress. The sysops of the Writers' Forum had
to lock her out of the chat rooms because she was filling
up the message boards with her off-topic ramblings, and a
bunch of us had to get unlisted phone numbers.

Even the people who just want computer or editorial
advice expect me to give away my time for free; they don't
understand that I, too, have to work for a living.

Oh well. Sorry for the flame. I guess you've hit one of my
hot buttons. <g>

Just so you know—a "flame" is a message from someone
who's pissed off and venting; my message is pretty mild
compared to some of the flames you see online. A "sysop"
is someone who manages a forum (short for system opera-
tor), and the <g> is an electronic grin. Since you can't see
the expressions on people's faces or hear the inflections of

their voices when chatting online, a lot of people use the
<g> or :-) (sideways smiley face) to show they're joking or
trying to be friendly when typing something that could be
misconstrued.

Tell you what: Just to show you I'm not a horrible person,
I'll let you ask me one question, which I'll answer to the
best of my knowledge. One question, one answer. Deal?

Beverly

Saturday, July 22, 1995 2:14 a.m.
From: Maximilian@miller&morris.com
To: BevJ@frederic_gerard.com
Subj: One Question

Beverly,

It's a deal, and thanks for the background on what all that
jargon means. I've been wondering what it all stands for
since I got online a few weeks ago, but have always felt too
stupid to ask about it in a public chat room.

And now . . . my question:

Are you happy?

Monday, July 24, 1995 5:21 a.m.
From: BevJ@frederic_gerard.com
To: Maximilian@miller&morris.com
Subj: Re: One Question

Maximilian:

Can't we go back to talking about what kind of computer I think you should buy? <g>

Am I happy? What sort of question is that? Are you sure you're not trying to come on to me?

If you're so intent on getting personal, why don't you just ask me where I grew up? What my major was in college?

What my favorite color is? What kind of food I like, books
I read, or even who gave me my first kiss?

Beverly

Monday, July 24, 1995 8:57 p.m.
From: Maximilian@miller&morris.com
To: BevJ@frederic_gerard.com
Subj: Re: One Question

Beverly,

Come on! A DEAL IS A DEAL!

Maximilian

Tuesday, July 25, 1995 6:53 a.m.
From: BevJ@frederic_gerard.com
To: Maximilian@miller&morris.com`
Subj: Re: One Question

Maximilian:

You're right, a deal is a deal. I'll answer your question on
one condition: you quit using your caps lock key when
you're typing messages online — people consider it rude
because it looks like you're shouting.

Beverly

Tuesday, July 25, 1995 10:31 a.m.
From: Maximilian@miller&morris.com
To: BevJ@frederic_gerard.com
Subj: One Answer

OK, Beverly. I'm waaaaitinnnnnng . . . <g>

Wednesday, July 26, 1995 7:12 a.m.
From: BevJ@frederic_gerard.com
To: Maximilian@miller&morris.com
Subj: Re: One Answer

And why do I get the feeling you're enjoying this?

All right. I'll answer your silly question. Of course I'm happy . . . mostly. No one is 100% happy, right?

Are *you* happy?

Beverly

Wednesday, July 26, 1995 9:22 a.m.
From: Maximilian@miller&morris.com
To: BevJ@frederic_gerard.com
Subj: One More Question

Beverly, (have I told you that's a pretty name?)

I would like to know what would make you 100% happy.

Max

Friday, July 28, 1995 11:52 a.m.
From: Maximilian@miller&morris.com
To: BevJ@frederic_gerard.com
Subj: Hello?

Beverly,

So where are you? It's been a couple of days and I haven't
heard from you. Did I breach another cyber rule or something with my last message?

Max

Friday, July 28, 1995 5:48 p.m.
From: BevJ@frederic_gerard.com
To: Maximilian@miller&morris.com
Subj: Re: Hello?

Maximilian:

No, you didn't breach any more cyber rules. I've had a lot
going on at work lately, trying to settle an ongoing dispute
between my writers and graphic designers. The writers are
upset because the designers keep typesetting their stories
in 6-point type, and the designers are upset because the
writers won't cut the copy to fit their pretty layouts. I've
finally gotten them to compromise: The designers agreed
to set the type in 8 points—still too small IMO—and the
writers agreed to cut ten lines of their precious copy.

Anyhow, getting back to our topic du jour, there's no way
I'm going to answer a second question from you! A deal is
a deal, remember? And besides, you never even answered
my question, about whether or not *you're* happy.

Beverly

Beverly,

I'm glad to know I haven't pissed you off again. I really like talking to you. You probably think I'm some geek who gets off on trying to pick up chicks online, but you're the only person I've "met" so far who seems to have half a brain.

Since I'm the one who started this whole damn thing, I guess I owe it to you to answer my own question. To tell you the truth, I'm not very happy at all—though it would surprise the people who know me to hear me say that. Most people think I'm a happy-go-lucky guy who happens to be a kick-ass advertising copywriter making a pretty damn good living.

I've been having a lot of problems at work lately and I guess that's the reason I'm not happy. The owner of my ad agency is a total maniac who goes around making people's lives miserable. We all joke about him behind his back, but when you get right down to it, I'm beginning to think he's eating me alive. This is a cutthroat business to begin with, so I never thought of myself as thin-skinned, but I'm wondering how much longer I can take it.

What bothers me the most is that my happiness seems to be so closely tied with who I am professionally. Why do so many of us value ourselves based on what we do for a

living—on whether our bosses give us a big raise or not
and how much our coworkers say they like us?

Ah, well. I didn't mean to get all philosophical on you. I
guess it's because it's two in the morning; I just got back
from a night on the town with some friends and I think
I've had one martini too many.

Maximilian

Monday, July 31, 1995 9:02 a.m.
From: BevJ@frederic_gerard.com
To: Maximilian@miller&morris.com
Subj: Job Stuff

No, I don't think you're a geek, Maximilian. In fact, as
much as I hate to admit it, I'm actually enjoying talking to
you, too. It's a nice break from some of the drivel I have to
deal with all day.

I'm sorry to hear about what you're going through at work.
I can honestly relate, because I had a boss like that once.
No corporate environment is ever perfect, but the last
place I worked added a whole new dimension to the term
"dysfunctional."

All I can tell you is that you've just got to keep doing what
you think is right. No matter what happens, you want to

be able to look at yourself in the mirror in the morning
and like what you see.

Take care,

Beverly

Monday, July 31, 1995 10:29 a.m.
From: Maximilian@miller&morris.com
To: BevJ@frederic_gerard.com
Subj: Re: Job Stuff

Beverly,

Thanks for the encouragement. So what happened at the
last place you worked? Did you quit?

Maximilian

p.s. If you won't tell me what would make you 100%
happy, maybe you could just tell me about your first kiss.
;-)

Tuesday, August 1, 1995 6:14 a.m.
From: BevJ@frederic_gerard.com
To: Maximilian@miller&morris.com
Subj: Re: Job Stuff

Maximilian:

Check you out — using emoticons! That sideways wink was pretty impressive. ;-)

To answer your question about the last place I worked, no, I didn't quit — I was fired. It happened during a big presentation we were doing for a bunch of senior executives. The design director and I were standing next to an easel at the front of the room, talking through a series of cover design comps. Halfway through the presentation the boss starts ranting about how he doesn't like the colors on any of the cover designs, and in the middle of his rant he glances down at my feet and happens to notice I'm wearing two different color socks that day. (One was navy blue and the other was sort of a hunter green. Apparently I was stressed out about the presentation while getting dressed that morning, because I'm normally a fanatic about color-coordinating my entire outfit — down to my socks, underwear, and nail polish.)

So anyway, the room goes silent, and the boss fires me on the spot, right there in front of everyone — because how in the world could I possibly have good taste in cover designs if I can't even match the color of my own socks?

It makes for a funny story now, but at the time I was pretty upset. Like you, my self-esteem back then was based largely on my professional accomplishments. I worked my ass off and, along with everyone else at the company, lived in a constant state of panic trying to please our nut job of a boss. We never knew who he'd find in his crosshairs from one day to the next, so when I finally got fired it was actually a huge relief. Turns out the reality of getting fired is a lot less horrible than living in nonstop fear of getting fired.

My mom used to quote Franklin Roosevelt when we were kids — "The only thing we have to fear is fear itself" — and boy, was she right.

Beverly

p.s. I can't tell you about my first kiss — I'd be too embarrassed, and besides, we hardly know each other!

Tuesday, August 1, 1995 10:58 a.m.
From: Maximilian@miller&morris.com
To: BevJ@frederic_gerard.com
Subj: First Kiss

CHICKEN!!! <g>

p.s. I hope you notice that, in the interest of gentlemanly behavior, I've refrained from commenting on your matching socks, underwear, and nail polish.

Tuesday, August 1, 1995 7:13 p.m.

> Writers' Forum   > Live Conference   > People Here: 19

DonA(Mod): For those who just joined us, the topic of tonight's live chat is how to find a job in advertising. We don't have a planned guest, so we'll be relying on audience members to contribute their expertise. First I'd like to briefly go over a few rules of live conference etiquette . . .

If you'd like to ask a question or make a comment, type ? (question mark) or ! (exclamation point). As the moderator, I'll tell you to go ahead with a GA followed by your name. If everyone behaves, I'll eventually dispense with the GAs and let you talk freely amongst yourselves.

ThomH: ?

DonA(Mod):   GA, Thom.

ThomH: Is there anyone here who already works in advertising?

BevJ: !

DonA(Mod):   GA, Bev.

BevJ: Maximilian is a copywriter—or so he claims. <g,d&r>

ThomH: ?

Maximilian: !

DonA(Mod):   GA, Thom, then GA Maximilian.

ThomH: Maximilian, are you really a copywriter?

Maximilian: My boss might disagree but yes, I'm a professional copywriter. (Thanks for your support Bev.) <g>

ThomH: I'll be graduating from Colorado State next spring, but I have no idea how to start looking for a job. Any thoughts?

Maximilian: Aside from the things your college
                placement office should be doing for you,
                like career fairs and resume workshops,
                you could start looking for a position as an
                intern. Agencies love to hire interns (cheap
                labor). You won't get rich, but you're sure
                to get some useful experience—and make
                some good contacts.

ThomH: Thanks. That's good advice. How did you
                get started in the biz?

Maximilian: I actually started out as a secretary. After
                college I couldn't find any internships in
                my city, but there were want ads for clerical
                help at some local ad agencies. I'd taken a
                typing class in high school (I type 90wpm),
                so it was a natural fit. And the female execs
                loved the idea of having a male secretary.
                <g>

ThomH: You've given me some great ideas Max.
                Where do you work now, and would I
                know any of the campaigns you've worked
                on?

Maximilian: I work for Miller & Morris advertising.
                Have you seen the Monster Brewery
                campaign? I was the creative director on
                that. I also write all the copy for the Olivia's
                Boutique catalogs.

ThomH: Hey that's cool! I love the Monster Brewery
                ads—totally hip. And the Olivia's Boutique

catalogs . . . so sexy. How do you keep from getting uh, you-know-what during the photo shoots? <g>

Maximilian: Who says I don't? <weg>

DonA(Mod):   OK guys, this is a family forum, remember?

BevJ: You're right Don. In fact I'm pretty sure Max is still going through puberty.

Maximilian: What do you mean — puberty? I'm already working on my mid-life crisis.

DonA(Mod):   We need to get back on topic here, gang.

ThomH: Maximilian, thanks again. I'll let you know how my interviews go.

Maximilian: For your own sake Thom, I hope you *don't* get a job in advertising. Get a nice career, like selling insurance. Or maybe you could be an editor like Bev. <g> Well folks, there's a martini chilling in my fridge and it's calling my name — gotta run.

ThomH: Bye Maximilian. Thanks again.

KT: Goodnight Max.

Maximilian: Ciao everyone!

%System%:   Maximilian has left the forum.

ThomH: Has anyone here actually met Maximilian?

KT: Why do you ask, Thom?

ThomH: Just wondering if he really did write that ad
                campaign.

KT: He's for real. We were both panelists at a
                writers' convention a few years ago. He's
                kind of a loose cannon when it comes to
                public speaking events, but with looks like
                that, who needs to know how to talk? ;-)

4

Wednesday, August 2, 1995 8:03 a.m.
From: BevJ@frederic_gerard.com
To: Maximilian@miller&morris.com
Subj: First Kiss

My first kiss was pretty gross. I was thirteen, and on my first date with a boy named Bill Jablonski. He took me to the Tulip Festival, our town's annual spring carnival. I had a huge crush on him, and like most thirteen-year old girls, I was both hopeful and terrified he'd try to kiss me good-night at the end of our date. In fact, that's pretty much all I could think about the entire night, so I don't remember much of the evening . . . except for what happened right before he kissed me.

He wanted to go on the Ferris wheel together, but I was afraid of carnival rides (yep, even one as mild as the Ferris wheel). So he went on it by himself while I stood on the ground looking up at him, waving and smiling. I think he was a little ticked at me for not going on the ride with him, but unfortunately he wasn't ticked off enough to change his mind about kissing me goodnight. I say "unfortunately" because Bill threw up in the bushes right after he got off the Ferris wheel. (Too much kettle corn and cotton candy I guess.)

He didn't seem too embarrassed, but I was mortified, and became even more so once I figured out he intended to kiss me goodnight. I mean, it wasn't like he had a toothbrush and a tube of Crest in his back pocket. I thought maybe I'd been saved when we saw his dad's car pull into the parking lot, but Bill laid one on me right before his dad got out of the car to greet us.

Bill was my second boyfriend. My first boyfriend broke up with me because I wouldn't let him kiss me—I only wanted to hold hands. After The Bill Experience, it took two more boyfriends before I'd even consider the idea of kissing again. By that time I was fourteen and going steady with Kurt Aurelio, who provided me with a whole new perspective on kissing. . . . <g>

Satisfied?

Wednesday, August 2, 1995 9:47 a.m.
From: Maximilian@miller&morris.com
To: BevJ@frederic_gerard.com
Subj: Re: First Kiss

Are you still afraid to go on the Ferris wheel?

Thursday, August 3, 1995 7:08 a.m.
From: BevJ@frederic_gerard.com
To: Maximilian@miller&morris.com
Subj: Re: First Kiss

No—I like riding the Ferris wheel now. But I still won't
go on the Tilt-A-Whirl.

Can we talk about something else now? <g>

Thursday, August 3, 1995 10:51 a.m.
From: Maximilian@miller&morris.com
To: BevJ@frederic_gerard.com
Subj: You

OK. Tell me what you look like.

Friday, August 4, 1995 6:11 a.m.
From: BevJ@frederic_gerard.com
To: Maximilian@miller&morris.com
Subj: Re: You

Absolutely not. In fact, you're starting to piss me off again
Maximilian. I have a husband, remember?

Friday, August 4, 1995 4:19 p.m.
From: Maximilian@miller&morris.com
To: BevJ@frederic_gerard.com
Subj: Re: You

OK. Tell me what your husband looks like.

Monday, August 7, 1995 6:32 a.m.
From: BevJ@frederic_gerard.com
To: Maximilian@miller&morris.com
Subj: Re: You

Funny. Let's talk about something normal—like, where
did you grow up?

Tuesday, August 8, 1995 11:05 a.m.
From: Maximilian@miller&morris.com
To: BevJ@frederic_gerard.com
Subj: Boring

Ah, you mean let's talk about something *safe*? All
right. . . .

Let's see. I was born in a suburb of Milwaukee. My dad
was an actuary so we had a decent amount of money. My
mom stayed at home and took care of my two sisters and
me until we all went to college. My childhood was normal
to the point of being boring.

Is it my turn to ask a question yet?

Wednesday, August 9, 1995 6:12 a.m.
From: BevJ@frederic_gerard.com
To: Maximilian@miller&morris.com
Subj: Not Boring

GA. (Not guaranteeing I'll answer, however.)

Wednesday, August 9, 1995 9:30 a.m.
From: Maximilian@miller&morris.com
To: BevJ@frederic_gerard.com
Subj: You

Why are you talking to me?

Thursday, August 10, 1995 8:46 a.m.
From: BevJ@frederic_gerard.com
To: Maximilian@miller&morris.com
Subj: Re: You

I don't know.

Thursday, August 10, 1995 9:14 a.m.
From: Maximilian@miller&morris.com
To: BevJ@frederic_gerard.com
Subj: Re: You

Bullshit.

I admit we don't know each other very well yet, Beverly, but I do know enough about you to know you're not the type of person who does things without a reason. So fess up. Why are you talking to me?

Thursday, August 10, 1995 5:37 p.m.
From: BevJ@frederic_gerard.com
To: Maximilian@miller&morris.com
Subj: Silly Me

You've pretty much answered your own question Maximilian. I'm talking to you because I don't have a reason for talking to you.

Beverly

Thursday, August 10, 1995 8:57 p.m.
From: Maximilian@miller&morris.com
To: BevJ@frederic_gerard.com
Subj: Huh?

::: shaking head :::

I don't understand.

Friday, August 11, 1995 8:42 a.m.
From: BevJ@frederic_gerard.com
To: Maximilian@miller&morris.com
Subj: Re: Huh?

You're right to say I'm the kind of person who does
everything for a reason. I've worked hard to get my life the
way I want it, and I'm proud of that. But sometimes I feel
like doing something just a little bit irrational. Talking
to a stranger online like this is something I wouldn't
normally do.

Friday, August 11, 1995 10:01 a.m.
From: Maximilian@miller&morris.com
To: BevJ@frederic_gerard.com
Subj: Re: Huh?

So why am I different?

I haven't figured that out yet.

Saturday, August 12, 1995 3:18 a.m.
From: Maximilian@miller&morris.com
To: BevJ@frederic_gerard.com
Subj: Macworld

Beverly,

I heard about a computer trade show called Macworld
being held in Boston later this month, and I was
wondering if you go to those sorts of things. Believe it
or not, I wasn't making it up when I first wrote you and
told you I was looking for a new computer. So I've been
thinking about going to a trade show and maybe buying
a Mac while I'm there. I've also heard some pretty hip
parties happen at these shows. <g>

Maximilian:

First off, if you decide to go to Macworld, do not—I repeat, do NOT—buy your computer there. It would be much better to go through your local dealer. That way you can also get tech support and maybe a better warranty. Having said that (assuming you've made up your mind you want a Mac over a PC), it's still a good idea to go to a trade show like Macworld. You can check out all the latest hardware and software on the show floor, and listen to a lot of tech experts give their not-so-humble opinions.

And yes, some of the parties are pretty good too. ;-)

Beverly

Oh, so you *do* go to these types of shows? Will you be going to this one?

I don't go to many of the computer-related shows, but I've gone to Macworld a couple times. It's a good show for promoting some of our authors' computer books. But I won't be able to make it this time. I have another big deadline coming up and, while I'd love to get away, I need to save my travel budget for some upcoming writers' conferences.

How about you? Have you decided to go?

Oh, too bad. I was hoping we could jump each other's bones or something. <g,d&rvvf>

Wednesday, August 16, 1995 7:32 a.m.
From: BevJ@frederic_gerard.com
To: Maximilian@miller&morris.com
Subj: Get Real

Maximilian:

For Chrissakes, I tell you a few personal things about myself and now you think I'm going to hop in the sack with you? And what about the so-called gentlemanly behavior you were crowing about a few messages back?

I knew I shouldn't have continued talking with you . . . <sigh>

Beverly

p.s. Besides, I thought you said I was probably a real toad?

Wednesday, August 16, 1995 11:29 a.m.
From: Maximilian@miller&morris.com
To: BevJ@frederic_gerard.com
Subj: Re: Get Real

Sorry. I knew you'd get upset with me when I wrote that. I'm a guy—sometimes I can't help myself. <sheepish grin>

Friends?

p.s. I'd still want to talk to you, even if you are a toad.

Thursday, August 17, 1995 6:43 a.m.
From: BevJ@frederic_gerard.com
To: Maximilian@miller&morris.com
Subj: Re: Get Real

Oh gee, how charitable of you—you mean you actually talk to ugly girls too? I am *soooo* impressed.

Beverly

Thursday, August 17, 1995 10:42 a.m.
From: Maximilian@miller&morris.com
To: BevJ@frederic_gerard.com
Subj: Re: Get Real

Come on, Bev. I'm sorry. And I wasn't making a joke when I said I'd still want to talk with you, no matter what you look like.

You know, you piss me off sometimes too.

Thursday, August 17, 1995 12:30 p.m.
From: BevJ@frederic_gerard.com
To: Maximilian@miller&morris.com
Subj: Re: Get Real

And why is that?

Thursday, August 17, 1995 1:44 p.m.
From: Maximilian@miller&morris.com
To: BevJ@frederic_gerard.com
Subj: Re: Get Real

Because you intrigue the hell out of me.

Thursday, August 17, 1995 3:38 p.m.
From: BevJ@frederic_gerard.com
To: Maximilian@miller&morris.com
Subj: Game?

Maximilian:

I find that hard to believe. Since we've started "talking"
to each other, I've told you more about myself than you've
told me about yourself.

I have an idea. How about if we play a little game?

Friday, August 18, 1995 1:00 a.m.
From: Maximilian@miller&morris.com
To: BevJ@frederic_gerard.com
Subj: Re: Game?

A little game of virtual strip poker perhaps?

KIDDING!!!

Seriously, what kind of game do you want to play?

Friday, August 18, 1995 7:53 a.m.
From: BevJ@frederic_gerard.com
To: Maximilian@miller&morris.com
Subj: Re: Game?

Tell me something you've never told anyone else before.

Friday, August 18, 1995 9:24 a.m.
From: Maximilian@miller&morris.com
To: BevJ@frederic_gerard.com
Subj: Re: Game?

Are you serious?

Friday, August 18, 1995 4:56 p.m.
From: BevJ@frederic_gerard.com
To: Maximilian@miller&morris.com
Subj: Re: Game?

Totally.

OK. Here goes. ::: taking deep breath :::

I've never been in love.

6

Sunday, August 20, 1995 12:59 a.m.
From: Maximilian@miller&morris.com
To: BevJ@frederic_gerard.com
Subj: Shit!

Beverly,

I can't believe I sent you that message last night. I feel like such a dork.

Can I retract it?

Maximilian

Monday, August 21, 1995 5:29 a.m.
From: BevJ@frederic_gerard.com
To: Maximilian@miller&morris.com
Subj: Re: Shit!

Maximilian:

No, you can't retract it — unless you've fallen in love over-
night? And no, I don't think you're a dork.

I admit I was surprised when I read your message, and I'm
still not quite sure what to say. (When in doubt, talk like a
therapist: "So, Max, how do you feel about that?")

Not to make light of things, but I guess I do want to know
if this is something that weighs heavily on your heart.

Bev

Monday, August 21, 1995 9:08 a.m.
From: Maximilian@miller&morris.com
To: BevJ@frederic_gerard.com
Subj: Re: Shit!

Bev,

I'm glad you don't think I'm a total dork. Sometimes I
think I must be if I've never fallen in love.

It's not as if I haven't been involved in my share of serious
relationships (and some not-so-serious ones too). I was

even engaged once, but broke off the relationship about six weeks before the wedding. (Yes, right after the invitations went out—what a jerk.)

I've never even said "I love you" to anyone but my parents—not even to my former fiancée, Tracy. Sometimes I wonder if maybe I *have* been in love but was just too stupid to recognize it. I guess it is something that bothers me.

What does it feel like to be in love?

Max

> *Tuesday, August 22, 1995 8:37 a.m.*
> *From: BevJ@frederic_gerard.com*
> *To: Maximilian@miller&morris.com*
> *Subj: Luv*

Max:

I suppose it's different for everyone. For most people, falling in love is probably just like in the movies—an adrenaline rush, like walking on air, head in the clouds—all that happy horseshit. For others, I imagine falling in love is more painful—angst, longing, heartache.

I admire that you've never lied and told someone you loved her when you didn't (as I'm sure you must've been tempted). On more than one occasion I've said "I love you too" when I knew damn well I didn't. I'm not sure why, because I think of myself as an honest person. It was probably to avoid an uncomfortable moment. Or get some gorgeous hunk in the sack. <g>

Why did you call off the wedding?

Bev

Tuesday, August 22, 1995 11:47 a.m.
From: Maximilian@miller&morris.com
To: BevJ@frederic_gerard.com
Subj: Re: Luv

One of the reasons was that it finally occurred to me how strange it was she still wanted to marry me even though I'd never said "I love you." Turns out she had her own things going on at the time which I didn't learn about until recently. I happened to run into Tracy last year, during Homecoming weekend at Marquette (where we both went to college). We ended up having a few drinks together, which was nice because it was the first time we'd been able to have a civilized conversation since the big wedding kerfuffle. So we get to talking and she finally comes out and tells me she's marrying her best friend, who happens to be the woman she was rooming with back in college. They weren't romantically involved while Tracy and I were dating, but Tracy had been struggling with her feelings right up to the point when I called off the wedding. In fact she thanked me for being the one to call things off. She said that even though she acted like a jerk about it at the time, she was secretly relieved. And it ultimately led to her getting together with her true love, she's never been happier, and . . . yadda yadda yadda.

I'm happy for her too, but that doesn't solve my own little mystery of why I haven't fallen in love yet.

And BTW, nice try on your answer to my question about what it feels like to be in love, Bev. Don't think I didn't notice you bullshitted your way through that with meaningless generalities. I'm not interested in what love feels like for *most* people. I want to know what it feels like to *you*.

Tuesday, August 22, 1995 5:29 p.m.
From: BevJ@frederic_gerard.com
To: Maximilian@miller&morris.com
Subj: Re: Luv

Busted. <g>

OK. For me, falling in love has always been a mixture of electricity and calm. The electricity comes from the chemistry and sparks and sexual attraction; the sense of calm is from feelings of fulfillment and peace.

Bev

Wednesday, August 23, 1995 12:04 a.m.
From: Maximilian@miller&morris.com
To: BevJ@frederic_gerard.com
Subj: Re: Luv

So you've been in love more than once?

Wednesday, August 23, 1995 7:28 a.m.
From: BevJ@frederic_gerard.com
To: Maximilian@miller&morris.com
Subj: Re: Luv

Yes.

Wednesday, August 23, 1995 9:06 a.m.
From: Maximilian@miller&morris.com
To: BevJ@frederic_gerard.com
Subj: Re: Luv

Do you love your husband?

Wednesday, August 23, 1995 12:51 p.m.
From: BevJ@frederic_gerard.com
To: Maximilian@miller&morris.com
Subj: Re: Luv

Yes.

Tuesday, August 29, 1995 7:07 p.m.

> Writers' Forum   > Live Conference   > People Here: 21

DonA(Mod): Hello everyone. The topic of tonight's live
chat is our semi-annual Macworld update,
in which our forum members who were
lucky enough to attend the show fill us in
on all the hot technology news, especially
news that's pertinent to the Writers'
Forum. Our special guest tonight is Beverly
Johnson, editor-in-chief at Frederic Gerard
publishing, who attended the show in

Boston this past weekend. Let's let Bev
tell us about all the interesting things she
saw, and then we'll open up the floor to
questions. Bev?

BevJ: Thanks Don, and hello everyone. Probably
the biggest excitement at the show was over
the new Power Macs—Apple's booth was
literally mobbed with people trying to get
a peek at the new models. Storage devices
were another hot item at the show, as were
authoring tools for the WWW.

JimD: ?

DonA(Mod): GA, Jim.

JimD: Did you go to any good parties?

BevJ: Yeah—the Fractal party was wild!

Kass: ?

DonA(Mod): GA, Kass.

Kass: Did you see the new Web layout application
called PageMill?

BevJ: Yep. It was a big hit at the show. Guy
Kawasaki called it "the PageMaker of the
'90s."

Maximilian: ?

DonA(Mod):   GA Maximilian.

Maximilian: I thought you said you weren't going to be
               at Macworld Bev?

BevJ: I know. I thought I wasn't going, but one of
               our editors got sick and my publisher sent
               me to fill in at the last minute. Did you go?

Maximilian: Yeah! It was great. I can't believe you didn't
               let me know you were going to be there.

BevJ: I thought about trying to contact you, but
               everything was so last minute, I forgot my
               PowerBook and had no way of sending
               email.

DonA(Mod)::   Ahem. Sorry to break up your little convo
               here guys, but can we get back on topic?

Maximilian: Oh, sure Don. Sorry. <g>

BevJ: Sorry Don! Does anyone else have
               questions about the show?

Nightwrtr: ?

DonA(Mod):   GA Nightwrtr—you're new to the forum,
               aren't you? Go ahead and introduce yourself
               to the rest of the group if you'd like before
               asking your question.

Nightwrtr: I just want to know what color underwear
                Bev is wearing.

BevJ: What the hell? Uh, Don, can you get rid of
                this guy?

DonA(Mod):   Just a sec . . . hold on everyone . . . AFK

%System%:   Nightwrtr has left the forum.

DonA(Mod):   Sorry about that Bev. I've locked him out of
                the forum.

Kass: What a creep.

BevJ: You can say that again Kass.

Kass: What a creep. <g>

BevJ: ::: going to fridge to get a beer :::

%System%:   Maximilian has left the forum.

Wednesday, August 30, 1995 1:40 a.m.
From: Maximilian@miller&morris.com
To: BevJ@frederic_gerard.com
Subj: Fine, Blow Me Off

Beverly,

I can't believe you didn't try to contact me before you left
for Macworld. In fact I'm kind of pissed. I thought we
were developing a friendship here—or is there some sort
of cyber etiquette that says you can't meet up with the
people you talk to online?

Maximilian

I guess you really are mad at me, since you've gone back to calling me Beverly instead of Bev. <g>

Now who's being a smartass?

Come on. Is there a reason you didn't even try to contact me?

Max:

Part of the reason was that I didn't have time—honest. I had to rush home from the office Wednesday afternoon

to pack, then rush from home to the airport to catch my
flight to Boston the same night.

Bev

Hmmmm. So you had to fly to Boston? I guess that
means you don't live there—or at least not within driving
distance. . . .

Maximilian, it says in my member profile I live in the
Midwest, remember? (And no, I'm not going to get any
more specific than that.)

Friday, September 1, 1995 11:58 a.m.
From: Maximilian@miller&morris.com
To: BevJ@frederic_gerard.com
Subj: Re: Fine, Blow Me Off

So what's the other part of the reason you didn't try to get
in touch with me?

Monday, September 4, 1995 12:01 a.m.
From: Maximilian@miller&morris.com
To: BevJ@frederic_gerard.com
Subj: Re: Fine, Blow Me Off

Hello? Bev? Are you there?

Tuesday, September 5, 1995 10:00 a.m.
From: BevJ@frederic_gerard.com
To: Maximilian@miller&morris.com
Subj: Re: Fine, Blow Me Off

Max:

I'm sorry I didn't write back sooner — since it was Labor
Day weekend, we went away for a few days. Besides, even
though I do have a computer and modem at home, I usually only log on from the office.

If you must know, the other reason I didn't try to contact you before I left for Macworld is because I was afraid to.

Bev

You've got to be kidding. Why would you be afraid to meet me in person?

Max

Because I was afraid of what might happen between us.

Wednesday, September 6, 1995 8:58 a.m.
From: Maximilian@miller&morris.com
To: BevJ@frederic_gerard.com
Subj: Re: Fine, Blow Me Off

Hot damn! You mean you actually *would* let me jump
your bones?! This is what I call progress! <g,d&r>

Thursday, September 7, 1995 8:11 a.m.
From: BevJ@frederic_gerard.com
To: Maximilian@miller&morris.com
Subj: Re: Fine, Blow Me Off

Sometimes I wonder why I keep talking with you.

Thursday, September 7, 1995 10:42 a.m.
From: Maximilian@miller&morris.com
To: BevJ@frederic_gerard.com
Subj: Re: Fine, Blow Me Off

Oh come on Bev. Lighten up. You know I was just kidding
around. Seriously now. What's there to be afraid of?

Well, a lot of things could go wrong if we were to meet
in person. And yes, I admit to feeling a certain attraction
toward you, and one of the reasons I was afraid to get
together was that the attraction might lead to something
complicated.

But what's more likely to happen when two people who've
been chatting online meet in person is that the whole
thing turns out to be anticlimactic and both people end
up feeling disappointed. Even if the two people are just
friends online and they meet as friends in person, the
reality can be wildly different from the online relationship.
What's worse, once two people have met F2F and they try
to return to the way things were online, the magic has all
but disappeared.

I've seen it happen dozens of times, Maximilian. Two
people get all hot and bothered over an online romance
that goes on for months, then they meet somewhere and
it's totally awkward and uncomfortable. The same thing
can happen even when two people are just friends. A few
years ago I developed a close online friendship with a
woman who'd been doing some freelance work for me.
She was smart and funny and we exchanged emails almost
every day. But then one time I met her for lunch in an
airport on my way through her town, and she totally got
on my nerves!

I mean, it wasn't her looks or anything about her physical appearance that put me off. It's just that things that seem benign in cyberspace can quickly become annoying in real life. I could tell from her emails she had a strong personality—maybe even a little on the zany side—but that was one of the things I liked about her. Except in person, she turned out to be abrasive and obnoxious. For one thing, I was embarrassed by how rude she was to our waitress. (You can tell a lot about a person by the way she treats the wait staff, you know?) And then, before I was even done eating, she lights up a cigarette and starts flicking the ashes onto the remains of her club sandwich!

On top of that, she didn't seem at all interested in anything I had to say. She just rambled on about herself and her freelance book packaging business during the entire lunch, and the fact that I was even there seemed secondary to her. It was odd because in her emails she didn't come off as self-centered and boorish like that. But by the end of the lunch I was asking myself if this was even the same person I'd been corresponding with all that time. When we resumed our talks via email, I couldn't stop picturing her cigarette ashes mixed with little pieces of lettuce and tomato and sourdough bread. It sounds silly now, but the friendship was never the same after that.

Don't get me wrong—these things don't always end badly. Two of our colleagues from the Writers' Forum met online, are now happily married and have two beautiful daughters. I'm sure they'll live a long and fulfilling life together. Several other people I know have had some pleasant flings with people they met online, and as for myself, I've made numerous friends in business forums who've become my friends in real life too.

But when it comes to you and me, Maximilian, I'm
not going to take the chance. I don't want to lose our
friendship.

Beverly

I think I can understand that.

On to lighter topics. Did you have a good time at
Macworld?

Friday, September 8, 1995 7:26 a.m.
From: BevJ@frederic_gerard.com
To: Maximilian@miller&morris.com
Subj: Macworld & Stuff

Maximilian:

Yeah, I had a good time at Macworld. It
was . . . interesting.

How about you? Did you have fun? Did you decide which
Mac you're going to buy?

And BTW, how's everything going with your job? Is the situation with your boss getting any better?

Friday, September 8, 1995 9:35 p.m.
From: Maximilian@miller&morris.com
To: BevJ@frederic_gerard.com
Subj: Re: Macworld & Stuff

I had a great time—what a fun show! I even made the rounds of parties, and at one of them they showed a preview for a new movie called "Toy Story," made entirely with computer graphics. As for which computer I'm going to buy, I'm still deciding between one of the new PowerBooks and a full-blown Power Mac. I like the idea of having a portable computer, so I'm leaning toward the PowerBook 5300, but I don't do a ton of traveling, so then I think I should get a Power Mac. (Really decisive here. <g>)

My boss is still a psychopath. What's worse, some wacko millionaire has decided to sue the agency for trademark infringement over an ad campaign written by Yours Truly. Now my boss has taken me off the account (it was a plum too—print campaign for Schmackhaft ice cream) and given it to some dweeb junior creative. So I'm in the shithouse even though the guy who's suing us doesn't have a leg to stand on. One of my lady friends in Accounting told me the agency was already hemorrhaging money, and now we're going to have to pay a wild pack of attorneys to defend us in this stupid lawsuit.

I'm thinking about changing careers altogether, because I don't think another agency is the answer. They're all nuthouses. A friend of mine who's an account exec at another of the big agencies here in town just lost his job this week—I guess the creative director and a bunch of other key players decided to jump ship and form their own agency, so half the accounts followed them. My friend's agency is now "downsizing" and he got laid off without even a severance package—just his last paycheck and a "don't let the door hit you in the ass on your way out."

Sorry for the flame-let. (Is that what you'd call a minor flame? <g>)

Thanks for letting me blow off some steam. I'm trying to not let the whole thing get me too depressed—putting things in perspective and all that. It's just a friggin' job, right?

Max

Monday, September 11, 1995 6:52 a.m.
From: BevJ@frederic_gerard.com
To: Maximilian@miller&morris.com
Subj: Ideal Job

You're welcome Maximilian. Anytime. <g>

I guess I'm pretty lucky because I'm finally happy with my job situation. I worked for a string of jerks early in my career, but somehow I seem to have found a place that allows me to do the best job I can with a minimum amount of bullshit.

What would be your ideal career? (And tell me about this "lady friend" of yours in Accounting!)

My lady friend in Accounting? She's the cutest little thing. About 5' 2", 100 lbs. soaking wet. Pixie haircut, big blue eyes. Did I mention she's like, 70 years old? Her name's Anne. We meet for tea breaks in the conference room. I keep her plied with Silver Needles and she gives me the lowdown on all the good gossip going around the agency.

As for my ideal job, I don't know. When I was a kid I wanted to be a professional hockey player. I was captain of my high school and college hockey teams, and we won all sorts of championships and I was pretty much a big stud. There was this smart-mouth kid on my high school team who was smaller than everyone else, and we used to give him so much shit, like stuffing him in his hockey bag and things like that 'cause he was such a jerk. Now he plays for the Blackhawks and is one of the highest paid players in the NHL.

I guess that goes to show things aren't always what they appear to be.

Now that I'm a grown-up, I think my ideal job would be
working as a UPS delivery guy. They get to drive those
big brown trucks all over town, wear shorts to work in the
summer, and if they get the right route, they can deliver
packages to all the hot women who work from home and
answer their doors in various stages of undress. ;-)

I guess since you already have the ideal job, I can't ask you
what yours would be. Geez—perfect job, perfect husband,
perfect life . . . what more could a girl want?

Tuesday, September 12, 1995 9:07 a.m.
From: BevJ@frederic_gerard.com
To: Maximilian@miller&morris.com
Subj: Re: Ideal Job

Ya know, I kinda hate it when people say stuff like that.
Like you said, things aren't always what they seem.

Wednesday, September 13, 1995 8:09 a.m.
From: BevJ@frederic_gerard.com
To: Maximilian@miller&morris.com
Subj: Getting to Know You

Maximilian:

I was wondering—what kinds of things do you do in your free time? I've noticed you log on a lot late at night on weekends. Your member profile says you write poetry and do bonsai gardening. Do you really?

Also, how can you drink martinis? Those things are gross!

Bev,

I love martinis—been drinking 'em since I was 12. (Just kidding.) You should hear me order a martini in a restaurant. It takes me several minutes to explain to the waitress exactly how I want it: Dry vodka martini on the rocks. Make that *very* dry—just wave the bottle of vermouth somewhere in the vicinity of the vodka. Not too many rocks. Chilled glass. Four anchovy olives. No anchovy olives? Forget it!

That's why I like going to my regular hangouts; they know exactly how to fix my martinis without me having to explain everything. I like getting the extra olives because then at least I've had something solid to eat with my drink. And between the olives and the anchovies, I'm covering two of the four food groups, right?

I used to write a lot of poetry, but haven't had much time lately (too busy dreaming up snappy tag lines I guess). I still do bonsai gardening though. I've got five bonsai trees on my balcony right now—one of them is eleven years old. It's a beaut.

Other than that, I do a lot of regular guy stuff like hanging out with my friends, watching hockey, and cruising the information superhighway. (And yeah, I do log on late at night. I'm a night owl, usually awake 'til two or three in the morning.)

How about you? Do you really study typography in your
spare time, or did you just put that in your profile to make
you look more intellectual? <g>

Max

Thursday, September 14, 1995 5:15 a.m.
From: BevJ@frederic_gerard.com
To: Maximilian@miller&morris.com
Subj: Re: Getting to Know You

Yes, I really do study typography in my spare time. My
home office is loaded with books on type, though I'm still
pretty much a novice. My goal is to someday be able to
recognize typefaces just by looking at them. As it is now,
I usually have to go through my type specimen books to
match a typeface to its name. Once in a while when we're
driving around town I'll recognize a typeface on a bill-
board and get all excited. My husband finds that amusing.

Mostly though, when I do have free time, my favorite way to spend it is reading. I'm your average book-
worm—always have my nose in something, with a stack
of new books on my nightstand waiting to be read. I like
biographies, mysteries, self-help, and computer books.
I used to play the piano—studied classical piano as a
kid—but I'm way out of practice. Someday I'd like to
study jazz piano and get a job doing a lounge act, so I can
wear sequined evening gowns and long black gloves to
work. <g>

And I suppose I'd better tell you here and now I'm a beer-drinkin' kind of gal. I never liked mixed drinks (especially martinis), but I do enjoy an occasional beer when we're out to dinner. (And none of that wimpy stuff either—I like brown ales, porters, and stouts.)

Thursday, September 14, 1995 10:04 a.m.
From: Maximilian@miller&morris.com
To: BevJ@frederic_gerard.com
Subj: Re: Getting to Know You

Hmmm. I've only met one other woman who likes the heavier beers. Myself, I prefer a drink that contains less foam and more alcohol. <g>

Self-help books? Why do you read self-help books? I mean, you don't strike me as the type. I thought you were more together than that.

Friday, September 15, 1995 5:36 a.m.
From: BevJ@frederic_gerard.com
To: Maximilian@miller&morris.com
Subj: Re: Getting to Know You

Well, it's not something I tell most people. I don't read as many of them as I used to. I think I OD'd on self-help books during one period of my life, and I admit a lot of the books I read back then were pretty useless. But some of them are helpful, and they do serve a purpose for lots of people. Most of the self-help books I read now have to do with positive thinking and stuff like that.

Can we change the subject? <g>

Friday, September 15, 1995 11:22 a.m.
From: Maximilian@miller&morris.com
To: BevJ@frederic_gerard.com
*Subj: Getting to Know *All* About You*

OK. I have an idea. . . .

Monday, September 18, 1995 8:13 a.m.
From: BevJ@frederic_gerard.com
To: Maximilian@miller&morris.com
*Subj: Re: Getting to Know *All* About You*

Oh God! You're having a brainstorm! Does it hurt?

(And from the way you changed the subject line of your email, something tells me I'm not going to like this idea of yours.)

Monday, September 18, 1995 9:40 a.m.
From: Maximilian@miller&morris.com
To: BevJ@frederic_gerard.com
Subj: Re: Getting to Know *All* About You

My, my. Aren't you the little comedienne.

Tuesday, September 19, 1995 5:53 a.m.
From: BevJ@frederic_gerard.com
To: Maximilian@miller&morris.com
Subj: Re: Getting to Know *All* About You

So what's your brilliant idea, Einstein?

Tuesday, September 19, 1995 10:16 a.m.
From: Maximilian@miller&morris.com
To: BevJ@frederic_gerard.com
Subj: Re: Getting to Know *All* About You

I want you to tell me something you've never told anyone
else before.

Wednesday, September 20, 1995 7:02 a.m.
From: BevJ@frederic_gerard.com
To: Maximilian@miller&morris.com
*Subj: Re: Getting to Know *All* About You*

Hey! Can't you think of something more original Mr.
Advertising Copywriter? That's my line!

Wednesday, September 20, 1995 10:36 a.m.
From: Maximilian@miller&morris.com
To: BevJ@frederic_gerard.com
*Subj: Re: Getting to Know *All* About You*

So sue me. Are you going to answer my question or not? I
answered yours — turnabout's fair play, right?

Thursday, September 21, 1995 7:45 a.m.
From: BevJ@frederic_gerard.com
To: Maximilian@miller&morris.com
*Subj: Re: Getting to Know *All* About You*

Can I think about it for a few days?

Thursday, September 21, 1995 10:18 a.m.
From: Maximilian@miller&morris.com
To: BevJ@frederic_gerard.com
*Subj: Re: Getting to Know *All* About You*

It would seem I have no choice but to wait.

Monday, September 25, 1995 7:17 a.m.
From: BevJ@frederic_gerard.com
To: Maximilian@miller&morris.com
*Subj: Re: Getting to Know *All* About You*

Max:

OK, I've been mulling it over all weekend, and have decided to give you your damn answer. This is something I've honestly not told another soul, and I can't believe I'm about to spill my guts to you, but . . .

I've had an affair.

Now I suppose whatever respect you might have had for me is completely lost.

<sigh>

Thursday, September 28, 1995 4:57 a.m.
From: BevJ@frederic_gerard.com
To: Maximilian@miller&morris.com
Subj: Hello?

Maximilian:

I knew it—you're upset with me, you hate me, you think
I'm a big flake. I haven't gotten a response from you in
four days and your silence is killing me.

Bev

Maximilian? Are you there? Please answer this message. Even if you want to say something mean to me, just say something, OK?

Bev

Beverly,

I can't believe you did that!!! What about your husband? I thought you guys were happily married. Why the hell did you go and do something stupid like have an affair?

Max

Saturday, September 30, 1995 9:12 a.m.
From: BevJ@frederic_gerard.com
To: Maximilian@miller&morris.com
Subj: Re: Hello?

Maximilian:

I can't believe you're berating me for having an affair when you've been trying to pick me up online for two months now.

Beverly

p.s. And besides, it wasn't a full-blown affair. It was more like a one-night stand.

Sunday, October 1, 1995 3:14 a.m.
From: Maximilian@miller&morris.com
To: BevJ@frederic_gerard.com
Subj: Re: Hello?

A one-night stand?! Bev, how could you do that? I simply cannot believe it.

And I haven't exactly been trying to pick you up. I mean, it's not as if I could jump through the modem and put my hand on your knee or anything. . . .

Monday, October 2, 1995 8:18 a.m.
From: BevJ@frederic_gerard.com
To: Maximilian@miller&morris.com
Subj: Harmless?

And I can't believe you're being so judgmental of me, like you're Mr. Perfect or something. I thought you'd be a little more understanding.

Monday, October 2, 1995 9:21 a.m.
From: Maximilian@miller&morris.com
To: BevJ@frederic_gerard.com
Subj: Re: Harmless?

Aww geez. I'm sorry. I'm just taken aback. I mean, you've really shifted my paradigm here Bev. <g>

I guess I had you on a pedestal, thinking of you as this perfect, untouchable woman, and I'm feeling kind of disappointed . . . and pissed . . . and jealous.

Tuesday, October 3, 1995 5:24 a.m.
From: BevJ@frederic_gerard.com
To: Maximilian@miller&morris.com
Subj: Re: Harmless?

Apology accepted. I'm feeling pretty disappointed in myself, too. It doesn't exactly fit in with my vision of who I'm supposed to be.

Tuesday, October 3, 1995 9:39 a.m.
From: Maximilian@miller&morris.com
To: BevJ@frederic_gerard.com
Subj: Re: Harmless?

So who was this guy anyway?

Wednesday, October 4, 1995 8:25 a.m.
From: BevJ@frederic_gerard.com
To: Maximilian@miller&morris.com
Subj: Re: Harmless?

I don't know.

Wednesday, October 4, 1995 10:47 a.m.
From: Maximilian@miller&morris.com
To: BevJ@frederic_gerard.com
Subj: Re: Harmless?

WHAT?!!! What do you mean YOU DON'T KNOW???

Wednesday, October 4, 1995 1:06 p.m.
From: BevJ@frederic_gerard.com
To: Maximilian@miller&morris.com
Subj: Re: Harmless?

Max,

Please quit shouting at me. I meant exactly what I said. I
don't know who he is. I met him at a party.

Bev

Wednesday, October 4, 1995 4:24 p.m.
From: Maximilian@miller&morris.com
To: BevJ@frederic_gerard.com
Subj: Re: Harmless?

OK, I'll stop shouting. But how could you meet a guy at a
party, sleep with him, and not know who he is?

Thursday, October 5, 1995 7:29 a.m.
From: BevJ@frederic_gerard.com
To: Maximilian@miller&morris.com
Subj: Re: Harmless?

I don't even know his first name.

Thursday, October 5, 1995 9:31 a.m.
From: Maximilian@miller&morris.com
To: BevJ@frederic_gerard.com
Subj: Fear of Flying

Oh that's just great. Fucking great. So, what . . . you think you're Erica Jong or something?

Friday, October 6, 1995 8:12 a.m.
From: BevJ@frederic_gerard.com
To: Maximilian@miller&morris.com
Subj: Re: Fear of Flying

Very funny Maximilian. You think you're real clever with your message header, don't you? (I didn't imagine you were the type to read erotic novels BTW. <g>)

Friday, October 6, 1995 10:56 a.m.
From: Maximilian@miller&morris.com
To: BevJ@frederic_gerard.com
Subj: Re: Fear of Flying

Thanks. I was pretty proud of myself when I came up with that. (I read my mom's copy of "Fear of Flying" when I was in junior high back in the '70s. She thought it was well hidden on the top shelf of the front-hall closet behind the hats and scarves, but leave it to a twelve-year old boy to sniff out mom's secret stash of dirty books.)

So, is there anything you *do* know about this guy?

Well, I guess that depends on what sorts of things you're talking about. I don't know his name, where he lives, what he does for a living, how old he is, or anything concrete like that.

I do know he was the most irresistible man I've ever encountered. I just couldn't help myself, Max. I'm ashamed to admit it, but it's true.

It happened at Macworld — at the Fractal party in the Boston Computer Museum. I was there by myself and everybody was doing the typical trade show routine: schmoozing, drinking wine out of clear plastic cups, nibbling on chunks of cheese, and pretending to be interested in the computer-generated artwork on the walls. I spotted him first — I think — and couldn't take my eyes off him. I mean, really. It was embarrassing. But not enough to make me stop looking at him. The cut of his charcoal gray suit, the fuchsia and violet colors in his linen tie, his crisp white shirt (incredible how fresh it looked after a long day on the show floor). His long, wavy black hair, strong nose (kind of big but in nice proportion with the rest of his face), olive skin, green eyes, long lashes. He had the most beautiful mouth — almost feminine-looking it was so perfect. His appearance was clean-cut and yet at the same time there was something about him that seemed . . . reckless. The guy exuded sensuality. Even from across the room, I could feel my body reacting to the sight of him. It was crazy. I've never had anything like that happen to me.

Not surprisingly, it didn't take long for him to notice me staring at him—I'm sure I was making a complete ass of myself. He smiled at me and then went back to looking at one of the digital paintings.

I can't explain what came over me, but I just started walking toward him. He saw me coming and smiled again, this time holding my gaze until I reached him. I said 'hi," and he said "hi." Silence. Usually at this point at these parties people start talking about who they work for and what they're doing at the show. But he began talking about the piece of artwork he was standing in front of, how much prettier it would be if it had actually been created with watercolors instead of in a software program. I agreed and told him there was some artwork along the opposite wall where the artist had used both digital media and oil paints. So we wandered around the museum, picking up cups of wine from the waiters and talking about each piece of art we came across.

We were so absorbed in one another we must have lost track of time, because suddenly the waiters were no longer walking around with their trays, the caterers had started packing up, and we were among the last people left at the party. By this time I was completely crazed over this man, and I could see he felt the same about me. It was chemistry of the most basic sort.

We stepped outside to the taxi line and when it was our turn for a cab we got into the back seat and I told the driver the name of my hotel. That was it. No conversation about a nightcap, no awkward invitations or pretending we had anything else in mind other than what we both clearly intended to do once we got back to my hotel room. We weren't even holding hands or sitting close to one another. But there was one hell of an electrical storm going on in the back seat of that taxi.

About halfway back to the hotel it occurred to me I didn't have any type of um, protection — and I didn't want to assume he had something that would cover it (so to speak <g>). So when we got to the lobby of my hotel, I gave him my room key and told him to go on ahead, I'd meet him up there in a few minutes. I headed to the little hotel store to buy a pack of condoms. The only ones they had were these godawful aquamarine ribbed things; it was so fucking embarrassing having to walk up to the 20-something cashier guy and pay for them. If only he knew. Here I was, a married woman, buying a pack of Trojans so I could have safe sex with some guy I'd met just hours ago. I was out of my mind.

But I'll tell you Max, every second of that night is permanently etched in my memory. I can't stop thinking about everything we did to each other. And I still don't know his name, and he doesn't know mine. He wanted to tell me, but I wouldn't let him. He wanted to continue the relationship — to see me again after that night — but I said no.

I know this doesn't make any sense, but I *am* happily married. My husband is a wonderful man and we still enjoy each other after all these years. It's not as if we're bored with one another or he treats me badly or anything like that. That's why I'm so torn up about the whole thing. I would never hurt my husband like that . . . or at least I thought I couldn't.

OTOH, I keep finding myself daydreaming about this man, wondering what he's doing, where he is, and if he's thinking about me too. At these moments I wish I'd taken his phone number so I could pick up the phone and call him and hear his voice. It's driving me crazy, Max.

Bev,

You must be going crazy, because I can see by your message headers you're logging online from home on the weekends now. You've always seemed so disciplined, judging from the times on your messages—I mean, logging on from the office at 5 a.m. on weekdays? Cripes! Now you're sending me messages on a Saturday morning from home, so I know you must be upset.

I'm not sure what to say. Are you asking me what you should do, or are you just looking for a sympathetic ear? I'm sorry I gave you such a hard time in the beginning; I'm trying to wrap my mind around the situation. I'll promise to be as good a friend to you as I can, but I can't guarantee I'll be much help.

Max

Thanks Max. I think I'm just looking for someone to talk to. Obviously there's no way I can talk about it with Gary, and I can't tell any of my friends about it either. I mean, they would totally freak out. I suppose the fact that you and I have never met F2F makes it a little easier for me to tell you these things.

Bev

Monday, October 9, 1995 9:20 a.m.
From: BevJ@frederic_gerard.com
To: Maximilian@miller&morris.com
Subj: Goddamn Guy

Max:

None of this really matters. I'll never see the guy again
anyway.

Maybe if I could just put the whole thing out of my mind
I could live with myself. You know, chalk it up as a Really

Stupid Mistake and forget about it. Get on with my life.
Go back to having fun and enjoying life with Gary.

But I can't.

Friday night Gary and I rented an old movie ("Rear
Window"—one of our favorites). It was late and we were
cuddled up next to each other on the couch eating Dove
Bars and watching the movie. We do this kind of thing a
lot on weekends. It's usually warm and intimate but, I have
to tell you, my mind and heart just weren't in it. I tried to
pay attention to the movie, but while I rested my head on
Gary's shoulder, all I could think about was the guy. The
Goddamn Guy whose name I don't even know.

I wonder if he thinks about me at all.

Bev

Monday, October 9, 1995 10:29 a.m.
From: Maximilian@miller&morris.com
To: BevJ@frederic_gerard.com
Subj: Re: Goddamn Guy

Bev,

Do you think Gary suspects something is wrong?

Max

I don't think so. I mean, there've been times in the past
when I've had things on my mind and I just kind of go
off in my own world for a while. But I always come back
to reality after a few days or weeks. I don't know how
I'm going to yank myself out of this one though. I'm in a
major black hole. I know this must all seem so stupid to
you.

No. It doesn't seem stupid to me Bev. I just wish there was
more I could do to help you through this.

Max

Wednesday, October 11, 1995 8:07 a.m.
From: BevJ@frederic_gerard.com
To: Maximilian@miller&morris.com
Subj: Re: Goddamn Guy

Just be my friend and let me continue confiding in you
without judging me. There's no one else in the world I
could tell these things to. It sounds so strange, but I really
need you right now.

Bev

Wednesday, October 11, 1995 10:40 a.m.
From: Maximilian@miller&morris.com
To: BevJ@frederic_gerard.com
Subj: Happy Birthday!

Hey Bev, isn't today your birthday? (It says so on your member profile.)

If so, HAPPY BIRTHDAY!!!

::: sending hugs across cyberspace :::

So what year were you born? <g,d&rvvf>

Max

Wednesday, October 11, 1995 4:43 p.m.
From: BevJ@frederic_gerard.com
To: Maximilian@miller&morris.com
Subj: Re: Happy Birthday!

Yep, today's the day. <sigh> I just wish I was in a better mood. Thanks for the wishes though.

::: returning hugs :::

I'm 36, in case you really wanted to know.

Bev

Thursday, October 12, 1995 2:04 a.m.
From: Maximilian@miller&morris.com
To: BevJ@frederic_gerard.com
Subj: Re: Happy Birthday!

Boy, you must be *truly* upset—you're answering my questions with straight-up answers. I didn't expect you to answer that question about your age—honest. I was just joking around.

But thanks. That's about the age I thought you were.

So, what can we talk about that will cheer you up? How about if I let you ask me a question — any question?

(I'm 32, in case you were wondering.)

Thursday, October 12, 1995 6:53 a.m.
From: BevJ@frederic_gerard.com
To: Maximilian@miller&morris.com
Subj: 20 Questions

OK, that sounds like fun. I'm trying to think of an interesting question . . . something that'll make you squirm. <eg>

I thought you'd be younger than that.

Thursday, October 12, 1995 10:35 a.m.
From: Maximilian@miller&morris.com
To: BevJ@frederic_gerard.com
Subj: Re: 20 Questions

I'll take that as a compliment. I think.

So what do you want to ask me?

::: squirming already :::

;-)

Friday, October 13, 1995 7:55 a.m.
From: BevJ@frederic_gerard.com
To: Maximilian@miller&morris.com
Subj: Boxers or Briefs?

Max,

As you can see from the subject line, I've come up with my question, and it's quite serious.

So tell me, do you wear boxer shorts or briefs?

Friday, October 13, 1995 11:48 p.m.
From: Maximilian@miller&morris.com
To: BevJ@frederic_gerard.com
Subj: Re: Boxers or Briefs?

My, aren't you getting bold these days. When we first started talking, you wouldn't even tell me if Beverly was your real name. Now you want to know what kind of underwear I wear?

Saturday, October 14, 1995 11:00 a.m.
From: BevJ@frederic_gerard.com
To: Maximilian@miller&morris.com
Subj: Re: Boxers or Briefs?

Yeah. Whatever. So are you going to answer my question or not? I thought you said you wanted to cheer me up?
<weg>

Sunday, October 15, 1995 3:38 a.m.
From: Maximilian@miller&morris.com
To: BevJ@frederic_gerard.com
Subj: Re: Boxers or Briefs?

Bev,

You sure know how to take advantage of a situation — talk about striking while the iron is hot! ;-)

I wear boxers. In fact I was wearing boxers way before it was cool to wear boxers. You know — Goldfish Theory and all that.

Monday, October 16, 1995 8:27 a.m.
From: BevJ@frederic_gerard.com
To: Maximilian@miller&morris.com
Subj: Re: Boxers or Briefs?

Hmmm. I pictured you as more of a briefs kind of guy. You know, like on the Calvin Klein ads. <g>

So what's this Goldfish Theory you're talking about?

Monday, October 16, 1995 10:49 a.m.
From: Maximilian@miller&morris.com
To: BevJ@frederic_gerard.com
Subj: Max's Goldfish Theory

Oh yeah—didn't I tell you I used to be a model for Calvin Klein before I became an advertising copywriter (and started wearing boxer shorts)? <vbg>

My Goldfish Theory. Well. Ahem. It's at the heart of every man's boxers-or-briefs dilemma. (And if more guys knew about my Goldfish Theory, they'd all switch to boxers.)

It has to do with the well-known fact that if you put a goldfish in a bowl that's too small, the goldfish will never get any bigger (and possibly even die a slow and painful death). So you should always keep your goldfish in the largest bowl possible. That way, your goldfish will have lots of room to grow.

Catch my drift?

Max

Tuesday, October 17, 1995 8:13 a.m.
From: BevJ@frederic_gerard.com
To: Maximilian@miller&morris.com
Subj: Re: Max's Goldfish Theory

Well. We certainly wouldn't want your "goldfish" to die a slow and painful death now would we?

Tuesday, October 17, 1995 10:24 a.m.
From: Maximilian@miller&morris.com
To: BevJ@frederic_gerard.com
Subj: Re: Max's Goldfish Theory

Well well well little missy. I hope you're having fun with yourself over there. <g>

Seriously, I'm glad I was able to cheer you up a bit.

Wednesday, October 18, 1995 8:34 a.m.
From: BevJ@frederic_gerard.com
To: Maximilian@miller&morris.com
Subj: Thanks

You have, Max. Thanks.

Bev

Wednesday, October 18, 1995 10:29 a.m.
From: Maximilian@miller&morris.com
To: BevJ@frederic_gerard.com
Subj: Re: Thanks

So does that mean you'll tell me what kind of underwear you wear?

Thursday, October 19, 1995 7:30 a.m.
From: BevJ@frederic_gerard.com
To: Maximilian@miller&morris.com
Subj: Re: Thanks

Not very likely.

Thursday, October 19, 1995 10:59 a.m.
From: Maximilian@miller&morris.com
To: BevJ@frederic_gerard.com
Subj: Re: Thanks

At least you didn't give me an absolute, flat-out no. . . .

}:-)

Friday, October 20, 1995 11:56 p.m.
From: Maximilian@miller&morris.com
To: BevJ@frederic_gerard.com
Subj: Hiya

Hi Bev,

So how are you doing?

Max

Ohhhh . . . OK, I guess. What are you up to?

Not too much. Trying to figure out some HTML stuff. Drinking coffee, bumming around. My usual Saturday morning antics.

Are you logging on from home or the office?

From home. Gary's away on a business trip, so I'm hanging out in my home office, aimlessly wading through the information ocean. :-)

So, what—are you going to create your own Web page or something?

Saturday, October 21, 1995 11:21 a.m.
From: Maximilian@miller&morris.com
To: BevJ@frederic_gerard.com
Subj: Re: Hiya

Yeah, I'm thinking about it.

We seem to be online at the same time. Why don't you give me your phone number—let me call you right now, so we can chat "live" and hear each other's voices?

Saturday, October 21, 1995 12:13 p.m.
From: BevJ@frederic_gerard.com
To: Maximilian&morris.com
Subj: Re: Hiya

No.

Saturday, October 21, 1995 1:06 p.m.
From: Maximilian@miller&morris.com
To: BevJ@frederic_gerard.com
Subj: Re: Hiya

Oooooookay. Guess you're pretty much opposed to *that* idea. <g>

So tell me something.

Saturday, October 21, 1995 3:17 p.m.
From: BevJ@frederic_gerard.com
To: Maximilian@miller&morris.com
Subj: Re: Hiya

Now what do you want to know? <g>

(Really. I've told you all my secrets. There's nothing interesting left to tell.)

Saturday, October 21, 1995 3:38 p.m.
From: Maximilian@miller&morris.com
To: BevJ@frederic_gerard.com
Subj: Re: Hiya

No, it's nothing that personal. I just want to know what you get from being online. I've been thinking about it myself lately, and I'm curious what people gain from this whole online thing.

Saturday, October 21, 1995 4:21 p.m.
From: BevJ@frederic_gerard.com
To: Maximilian@miller&morris.com
Subj: Junkie?

That's a fairly easy question, compared to the ones you've been asking me. <g> I'll give it a shot.

I originally got online because I had to. Several years ago I had a boss who was really into CompuServe, so the

whole editorial department had to get accounts and learn
our way around. At first I found dealing with modems
and telecomm protocols extremely frustrating. But once
I overcame the initial setup and got things working, I
was hooked. I got my current book publisher turned on
to email and the Internet and now we're even starting to
build a Web page showcasing our book catalog.

For me personally, I get a real charge out of chatting with
people from all over the place. I like hearing about what
people on the other side of the world are doing and thinking and reading, and logging on to the Net or CIS helps
me keep my finger on the pulse of things. I even log on to
AOL occasionally (although the ratio of creeps to profes-
sionals seems to be higher over there).

I'm sure there's more to it than that though. Sometimes I
think I'm turning into a communications junkie. No—let
me take that back. I've *always* been a communications
junkie. Except before, I'd write letters and talk on the
phone with friends for hours on end. Now all I have to do
is log on to some forum or newsgroup and I'm instantly in
the middle of a communications orgy. <g>

How about you? Why did you get online?

Saturday, October 21, 1995 5:33 p.m.
From: Maximilian@miller&morris.com
To: BevJ@frederic_gerard.com
Subj: Re: Junkie?

I admit my getting online had little to do with work or professional improvement. Mostly it was something like penis envy — my friends would be sitting around talking about their 14.4 or 28.8 baud modems and I was starting to feel a little left out. <g> I mean, we used to hang out in bars and talk about chicks and cars and sports, and now everyone's talking about modem speeds, hard drives, and RAM.

Remember the 1970s Corvettes — the ones with the really long front ends? We used to call those Penis Extenders. Nowadays a lot of the guys I know drive minivans. But being men, we've still got to have our Penis Extenders. So instead of Corvettes, now we go out and buy shit-hot computers with CD-ROM drives, 32-bit color, and more memory than we could ever dream of using.

Me, I'm now the proud owner of a *screamingly* fast 28.8 modem. (But I still have my old '386.)

Saturday, October 21, 1995 6:50 p.m.
From: BevJ@frederic_gerard.com
To: Maximilian@miller&morris.com
Subj: Re: Junkie?

Sounds like maybe you're not so worried about the size of your goldfish after all. ;-)

Saturday, October 21, 1995 8:41 p.m.
From: Maximilian@miller&morris.com
To: BevJ@frederic_gerard.com
Subj: Re: Junkie?

You got that right! ;-)

Wednesday, October 25, 1995 8:57 a.m.
From: BevJ@frederic_gerard.com
To: Maximilian@miller&morris.com
Subj: Just Checking In

Max:

Haven't heard from you in a few days and am wondering if you're all right.

Everything here is OK. Work's going well. Gary's fine. I'm still pretty much in a complete twist over the Goddamn

Guy, but am trying to get over it by focusing on other
things. (Not having much luck though.)

Hope everything's fine with you.

Bev

Thursday, October 26, 1995 11:07 a.m.
From: Maximilian@miller&morris.com
To: BevJ@frederic_gerard.com
Subj: Re: Just Checking In

So you've still got that Goddamn Guy on your mind, huh?
He must have been one helluva dude.

Everything here sucks. I think I'm going to get fired. As I
told you, things weren't going exactly swimmingly at work
to begin with. Then I kinda went on this minor bender
and missed the last three days of work.

When I came in this morning, people were avoiding me
in the hallways and whispering amongst themselves. Even
Anne from Accounting said she was too busy to meet me
in the conference room for tea.

I'm pretty sure my ass is grass.

Max

Thursday, October 26, 1995 12:12 p.m.
From: BevJ@frederic_gerard.com
To: Maximilian@miller&morris.com
Subj: Re: Just Checking In

What do you mean, you "kinda went on this minor bender and missed the last three days of work"? You call that "minor"?

Max, what's wrong? Something else besides work must be bothering you.

Bev

Friday, October 27, 1995 10:18 a.m.
From: Maximilian@miller&morris.com
To: BevJ@frederic_gerard.com
Subj: Re: Just Checking In

I *have* been pretty depressed lately Bev, but I didn't want to dump it on you since you were having your own troubles.

Max

Friday, October 27, 1995 4:36 p.m.
From: BevJ@frederic_gerard.com
To: Maximilian@miller&morris.com
Subj: Re: Just Checking In

Maybe it would be good for me to forget about my own problems for a while and try to help someone else. What's up?

I take it you haven't been fired yet, seeing as you're still logging on from work.

Bev

Saturday, October 28, 1995 1:06 a.m.
From: Maximilian@miller&morris.com
To: BevJ@frederic_gerard.com
Subj: Luv Sucks

No, I haven't been shit-canned yet. I did get called into my boss's office yesterday, and he screamed at me for an entire hour. I deserved a dressing down-for not showing up to work for three days, but the guy went completely overboard, name-calling and stupid shit like that. If I didn't know any better I'd say he gets off on humiliating people. What a fucking creep.

But that's not why I'm upset.

Well, I'm not saying you deserved to be called names or
yelled at for an hour, but not showing up to work for three
days is pretty serious. He could have fired you for that if he
wanted to, right?

So what's this really about? From your message header, I'm
guessing you're having some sort of romantic difficulties?

Right, and right.

So what the hell is going on? Are you going to make me
keep guessing?

And how can you say "Luv Sucks" if you've told me you've
never been in love before?

Bev

Saturday, October 28, 1995 6:01 p.m.
From: Maximilian@miller&morris.com
To: BevJ@frederic_gerard.com
Subj: Forget It

Because I've changed my mind.

Look, Bev. I'm having second thoughts. Maybe we
shouldn't talk about this right now.

Max

Saturday, October 28, 1995 6:54 p.m.
From: BevJ@frederic_gerard.com
To: Maximilian@miller&morris.com
Subj: Re: Forget It?

What do you mean you've changed your mind? You've
changed your mind about whether or not love sucks, or
whether or not you've ever been in love?

You can't back out now, mister. We're going to talk about
this.

I've got an idea—how about if we have a live chat?

Saturday, October 28, 1995 7:23 p.m.
From: Maximilian@miller&morris.com
To: BevJ@frederic_gerard.com
Subj: Re: Forget It?

You mean you'll let me call you?

Saturday, October 28, 1995 7:42 p.m.
From: BevJ@frederic_gerard.com
To: Maximilian@miller&morris.com
Subj: Re: Forget It?

No, I mean we can chat live *online*. As opposed to send-ing emails back forth, if we have a real-time chat we'll be able to instantly see what the other person types in the little dialog box as soon as they hit the return key. How about if you meet me in the Writers' Forum at 9 p.m. EST? When I see you've logged on, I'll initiate a private chat session — no one else will be able to see our conversa-tion except you and me.

OK?

Saturday, October 28, 1995 8:05 p.m.
From: Maximilian@miller&morris.com
To: BevJ@frederic_gerard.com
Subj: Re: Forget It?

OK. See you there.

Saturday, October 28, 1995 9:02 p.m.

> Writers' Forum > Live Chat > People Here: 2 > Private

BevJ: So you made it.

Maximilian: Yeah — this is pretty wild. How come we
never did this before?

BevJ: Dunno.

Maximilian: It's kind of like the live conferences, except
this is totally private, right?

BevJ: Right.

Maximilian: What do I do if I have to go to the
                bathroom or go get a martini?

BevJ: You just type AFK (Away From Keyboard).
                Then the other person will know you're
                not at your computer and it may be a while
                before you respond. I use it a lot when I'm
                online and my phone rings—I just type
                AFK and the other person knows I won't be
                typing for a few minutes.

Maximilian: I can see where this could become
                addicting. My bills for online time are
                going to get higher by the minute.

BevJ: Yeah, that's one of the drawbacks of live
                chats—the clock keeps ticking while you're
                typing. It's much less expensive to compose
                messages offline and send them all in one
                session.

Maximilian: Although talking live like this would seem
                to be a much better way to have cybersex.
                ;-)

BevJ: I wouldn't know.

Maximilian: So you're telling me you've been online
                all these years and you've never done the
                cybersex thing?

BevJ: Nope. Until my recent incident, I've always
                been faithful.

Maximilian: So let's talk more about that.

BevJ: Max, we didn't come here tonight to talk
                about me—we're supposed to be talking
                about you and your situation. So tell me
                what's going on?

Maximilian: Wellll . . .

BevJ: Hello?

BevJ: Max?

Maximilian: OK. <deep breath> Remember when I told
                you I've never been in love before?

BevJ: Yeah.

Maximilian: I think I've fallen in love with someone
                since then.

BevJ: You're kidding! How come you didn't tell
                me you'd met someone?

Maximilian: Lots of reasons, I guess. I always worried
                that I wouldn't recognize being in love
                when it happened, but it has finally
                happened and I'm completely in love. I
                mean, this is it. She's the one. I love this
                woman.

BevJ: Wow! I'm happy for you Max. What's she
               like?

Maximilian: She's beautiful. And I don't mean just
               her looks. She's smart. She's funny. She's
               compassionate, she's together, and she's
               absolutely *wicked* in bed. }:-)

               I worship her.

BevJ: So what's the problem?

Maximilian: She won't let me call her.

BevJ: Well that's weird. Is she not in love with
               you?

Maximilian: I think she is. She hasn't admitted it, but I
               think she's in love with me too.

BevJ: Are you sure this woman's not just leading
               you on Max?

Maximilian: I'm sure.

BevJ: Then why won't she let you call her?

Maximilian: Part of it is that I don't have her phone
               number.

BevJ: You've been sleeping with a woman yet you
               don't have her phone number? I don't get it.

Maximilian: We were only together one night.

BevJ: Ha! And here you were giving *me* shit
                 about having a one-night stand! So I guess
                 we can call it even now?

Maximilian: I met her at Macworld. At the Fractal
                 Party. The Boston Computer Museum. She
                 wouldn't tell me her name, or let me tell her
                 mine. But it was the most beautiful night of
                 my life. I love her.

Maximilian: Bev?

Maximilian: Are you there?

BevJ: You son of a bitch.

Maximilian: Bev, I know it was you. I'm in love with
                 you. Can't we just meet somewhere and talk
                 about this? Won't you at least let me call
                 you? I love you and I want to be with you.
                 This is making me crazy. I can't sleep. I
                 can't do anything at work. All I want to do
                 is sit at my computer and wait for your next
                 message.

BevJ: Max, stop.

Maximilian: I dream about the night we spent together.
                 It was perfect. Your body is perfect. Your
                 mind is perfect. I want to know everything
                 about you. I can still remember the smell
                 of your perfume. I even stole the pillowcase
                 from your hotel room, so I can smell you

every night when I try to go to sleep. But all
I do is lie awake and think about you.

BevJ: So that's where the pillowcase went. . . .

                 I can't believe this is happening.

Maximilian: Bev, I—

BevJ: Stop it Max! I don't want to hear it! You
                 goddamned son of a bitch. How long have
                 you known it was me? And you let me
                 make a fool of myself, let me go on about
                 my innermost feelings without knowing it
                 was you? YOU FUCKING ASSHOLE!!!!!!

Maximilian: Bev, I swear I didn't know it was you right
                 away. I only realized it was you when you
                 began telling me the details of the night we
                 spent together. I didn't even *ask* you for
                 details—you volunteered them! But once
                 I read your message describing the night
                 we spent together, there was no turning
                 back. I didn't know what to do. You said
                 you needed me to be your friend. I didn't
                 want our online friendship to end because
                 then I'd lose you completely. So I decided
                 to just not say anything. But then it reached
                 a point where I couldn't take it any longer. I
                 swear I wasn't trying to make a fool of you,
                 Bev.

                 I love you.

BevJ: I don't want to talk about this anymore. I
                 have to go Max.

Maximilian: No Bev! Please—don't go.

%System%:   BevJ has left the forum.

glossary

This list reflects Internet terms commonly used in the 1990s.

acronyms & abbreviations

AFAIK	as far as I know
AFK	away from keyboard
AOL	America Online
BG	big grin
BPS	bits per second
BTW	by the way
CIS	CompuServe Information Service
CO	live online conference
CUL	see you later
CULA	see you later alligator
F2F	face-to-face
FWIW	for what it's worth
FYI	for your information
G	grin
G,D,&R	grinning, ducking, & running
G,D,&RVVF	grinning, ducking, & running very very fast
GA	go ahead

GMTA	great minds think alike
HTML	HyperText Markup Language
IANAL	I am not a lawyer
IIRC	if I remember correctly
IMA	I might add
IMHO	in my humble opinion
IMNSHO	in my not-so-humble opinion
IMO	in my opinion
IRT	in regard to
JK	just kidding
LOL	laughing out loud
Net	short for Internet
NVM	nevermind
OMG	oh my God
OTOH	on the other hand
PMFJI	pardon me for jumping in
RL	real life
ROFL	rolling on floor laughing
ROFLOL	rolling on floor laughing out loud
RSN	real soon now
TIA	thanks in advance
TTYL	talk to you later
TPTB	the powers that be

VBG	very big grin
Web	short for World Wide Web
WEG	wicked evil grin
WRT	with respect to
WWW	World Wide Web

emoticons & other symbols

:-)	smile
;-)	wink
:-(	frown
:-*	kiss
:'-(	crying
}:-)	horny smile
:-O	surprised
< >	indicates an action <sigh>
::: :::	also indicates action ::: going to get body oil now :::
>>>>	used when quoting from another message
* *	signifies italics/emphasis in text
_ _	also signifies italics/emphasis in text

acknowledgments

This new 2014 edition features fresh cover and interior designs by David High of High Design. David designed the original, self-published editions of *Chat, Connect, & Crash* back in 1995, and I'm delighted he agreed to work with me again on the new edition.

I'm grateful to my copyeditor Faith Simmons for her attention to detail and fresh perspective, which helped ensure the updated *Chat, Connect, & Crash* manuscripts were publication-ready. Any remaining errors are my own.

Thanks to Kevin Callahan of BNGO Books whose professional typesetting, page composition, and ebook adaptation skills allowed me to stay focused on my writing. Anyone who says it's easy to self-publish a book is either lying or doing a shitty job. Authors need people like David, Faith, and Kevin to make sure we don't leave the restroom with toilet paper stuck to our shoes.

As in previous editions I'd like to once again acknowledge Wayne Sirmons, who provided early inspiration for the trilogy, as well as Laura and James Haggarty, one of the original "cyber couples" who met online in the late 1980s and who also served as inspiration.

Finally, thanks to my husband Pat (who provided real-life inspiration for Max) and our sons Ben and Coleman (you can wait until I'm dead to read the sex scenes) for their love and support.

Nan McCarthy is the author of the *Since You Went Away* series, *Chat, Connect, & Crash series, Live 'Til I Die,* and *Quark Design.* A former magazine editor and tech-industry writer, Nan founded Rainwater Press in 1992 and began selling her books online in 1995. The originally self-published *Chat, Connect, & Crash* series was acquired by Simon & Schuster in 1998. Nan regained the rights to the series and released new editions under the Rainwater Press imprint in 2014. Nan and her husband, a veteran who served 29 years in the Marine Corps, are the proud parents of two adult sons.

You can find Nan online in the following places:

nan-mccarthy.com

instagram.com/nanmccarthy

facebook.com/nanmccarthywriter

pinterest.com/nanmccarthy

twitter.com/nanmccarthy

amazon.com/author/nanmccarthy

also by nan mccarthy

fiction

Since You Went Away, Part One: Winter

Since You Went Away, Part Two: Spring

Since You Went Away, Part Three: Summer

Since You Went Away, Part Four: Fall

Chat: book one

Connect: book two

Crash: book three

non-fiction

Live 'Til I Die: a memoir of my father's life

Quark Design